"Ug-ly!"

"What do you call those things?" Felicity asked.

"I call them my shoes," said Priscilla. "I picked them myself."

"You picked those?" said Felicity. "I've got news for you. Those are the ugliest shoes I have ever seen. Ug-ly!"

Priscilla's feet turned to stone. Her cheeks burned. She stared at the beautiful shoes she had picked out herself. They looked gigantic. They looked ugly.

BEST ENEMIES

KATHLEEN LEVERICH
illustrated by Susan Condie Lamb

BULLSEYE BOOKS • RANDOM HOUSE
NEW YORK

FOR WALTER

Contents

I. Priscilla, Meet Felicity

That September morning Priscilla woke up early. "Hurry and dress," said her mother. "You do not want to be late for the first day of school."

Priscilla washed her face. She brushed her teeth. She put on her favorite dress. She put on her socks and her shoes. She opened her drawer, took out her brand-new pencil case, and zipped it open. Inside lay a pink eraser, a blue ballpoint pen, a red marker, and two yellow pencils with sharp points. Priscilla zipped the case shut and carried it downstairs to breakfast.

"Rrrrruf," barked her dog Pow-wow.

"Don't you look nice," said her mother.

"A regular little schoolgirl," said her father.

"Big deal," said her older sister Eve. "Would somebody please pass the orange juice?"

Priscilla felt a little nervous. "What if none of my friends are in my class?"

"Wrrouu," yipped Pow-wow.

Her mother placed a bowl of cereal in front of Priscilla. She gave her a hug. "Then you will meet new friends."

Priscilla was not so sure.

Priscilla and her mother read the class lists that were posted in the school's front hall.

"There is my name!" Priscilla pointed to the fourth list. "Priscilla Robin."

"Ms. Cobble's class," read Priscilla's mother. "Room 7."

"Is Jill in my class?" asked Priscilla.

"No," said her mother.

"Is Sue in my class?" said Priscilla. "Is Dennis?"

"I am afraid not." Rebecca's mother was looking down the list, too. "Here is a nice name, 'Felicity Doll.' She sounds like a brand-new friend."

Ms. Cobble stood in the doorway to Room 7. "Good morning." She shook hands with Priscilla's mother. "Good morning." She shook hands with Priscilla. "What a lovely new pencil case!"

Ms. Cobble gave Priscilla a big name tag to hang around her neck. "Go right inside," she told Priscilla. "Choose an empty desk and sit down."

Priscilla kissed her mother goodbye. She stepped into the classroom. Lots of boys and girls chattered in the room. Priscilla felt too shy to look at them carefully. She held her pencil case tightly. She looked at the desks.

Most of the desks had a flat top and an opening at one end where you could slide books inside. A few desks looked different. They were big and old. They were made of wood and had slanted tops. The tops opened upward like the top of Priscilla's toy chest. Priscilla watched a boy put his books inside one of those desks. He lifted the desktop high.

"Wow!" thought Priscilla. "I would like one of those desks with the slanty tops." She looked around the classroom. She saw an empty desk near the blackboard. It had a flat top. She saw an empty desk near the coat closet. It had a flat top. She saw an empty desk near the front of the room. It was big and old. It was made of wood and it had a slanty top. Priscilla hurried to the desk. She pulled out a chair and sat down.

"Hey!" said a voice.

Priscilla turned. Beside her stood a curly-haired girl. She wore a ruffly dress. The name on her name tag was too difficult for Priscilla to read.

"You will have to move," said the curly-haired girl. "This desk belongs to me."

Priscilla felt uncertain. Then she felt mad. "This desk was empty when I sat down," she told the curly-haired girl. Priscilla opened the desk. She put her pencil case inside. Beside it she put her lunch box. "This desk is mine."

The curly-haired girl looked at the pencil case. She looked at the lunch box. She smiled a snakey smile at Priscilla. "We could share this desk. Sharing would be the fair thing to do."

"I don't want to share," said Priscilla.

The curly-haired girl poked her in the chest. "Let me share this desk, or I will tell Ms. Cobble you are being selfish."

Priscilla pushed the curly-haired girl's finger away. "All right. But just for now."

"Oh, boy!" said the girl. She dragged up a chair. She jammed it next to Priscilla's. "Move over!" Priscilla had to sit so that one leg was under the

desk and one leg was outside it.

At the front of the room Ms. Cobble clapped her hands. "Let's settle down, class."

"Hey," the curly-haired girl nudged Priscilla. She pointed to Priscilla's name tag. "What does that say?"

"Priscilla," she said. She looked at the curly-haired girl's name tag. "What does yours say?"

14

The curly-haired girl fluffed her curls. "Don't you know how to read?" She pointed to her tag and spelled, "F-e-l-i-c-i-t-y. Felicity Doll."

Ms. Cobble handed out paper. She handed out crayons. She said, "Now, class—"

Felicity raised her hand. "Ms. Cobble!" She waved her hand as hard as she could. "Ms. Cobble!"

"Is something wrong, Felicity?" said Ms. Cobble.

Felicity squirmed in her seat. "I cannot work very well. Priscilla is crowding me."

Ms. Cobble walked over to where they sat. "What are you two girls doing at the same desk? There are plenty of empty ones. Come, Priscilla. We'll find you a desk of your own."

"But—" said Priscilla.

"Come along," said Ms. Cobble. "We have more things to do this morning than choose desks." She led Priscilla to an ordinary desk with a flat top in the very back row of the classroom. "Now," she said.

"Aren't you more comfortable at a desk of your own?"

"Ms. Cobble!" Felicity waved her hand. "Priscilla left this stuff in my desk." She took out Priscilla's lunch box and pencil case and carried them back to Priscilla's new desk.

"Thank you, Felicity," said Ms. Cobble. "I can see that you are going to be an outstanding Class Helper."

Ms. Cobble returned to the front of the room. Felicity returned to her seat.

"Now, class," said Ms. Cobble.

Felicity turned around. "Hey, Priscilla!" she whispered.

"What?"

Felicity stuck out her tongue. She covered her mouth and laughed a silent laugh.

"How was your first day of school?" said Priscilla's father that night at dinner.

"Terrible," said Priscilla.

"Rrrrgrrrr." Pow-wow lay under the table at her feet.

"Did you make new friends?" asked her mother.

"I made a new enemy," said Priscilla. "Her name is Felicity Doll. She stole my desk."

"Felicity Doll?" said Eve. "I know Felicity Doll. Felicity Doll is a real snake."

"Eve!" said Priscilla's mother. She was serving the salad. "I am sure Felicity is a lovely girl, once you get to know her."

Eve shook her head. "The one thing worse than having Felicity Doll for an enemy would be having Felicity Doll for a friend."

"I do not need to worry about that," Priscilla said.

The next morning when Priscilla arrived at school she found Felicity waiting beside her desk.

"This is an okay desk," said Felicity. "But my desk is much nicer."

"You stole that desk from me," said Priscilla. She sat down in her chair. She took her pencil case out of her desk. She took out a piece of paper and began to copy the new words Ms. Cobble had written on the blackboard.

Felicity stood beside Priscilla's desk. "Don't be mad, Priscilla. It is not my fault that Ms. Cobble made you move." Felicity leaned on the desk. "I like you, Priscilla."

Priscilla looked up from her paper. She could not believe her ears.

Felicity grabbed Priscilla's hand and squeezed it. "Be my friend. You can sleep over at my house. You can sit next to me at my birthday party. . . ." Felicity smiled her snakey smile.

"I have never slept over at a friend's house," said Priscilla. "My sister Eve goes on sleep-overs all the time."

"I have canopy beds," coaxed Priscilla. "I have a color TV in my room. . . ."

Priscilla freed her hand from Felicity's. "Canopy beds?" Perhaps Felicity was not so bad. "Very well," she said. "I will be your friend."

"Oh, boy!" said Felicity. "Now we can swap

pencil cases." She grabbed Priscilla's brand-new pencil case. She pulled her own case from her pocket and dropped it on the desk.

Felicity's case was a mess. The zipper was broken. Inside were two stubby pencils with chew marks. Nothing else.

"I do not want to swap," said Priscilla.

"Just for today." Felicity smiled her snakey smile. "Friends share."

Brnnnggg! The bell rang.

"So long, pal," Felicity took Priscilla's pencil case and hurried to her desk.

"Felicity!" Priscilla started after her.

"Priscilla, school has begun!" clapped Ms. Cobble. "No more visiting with Felicity. Sit down."

Priscilla sat.

"Now, class," said Ms. Cobble.

Felicity turned around at her desk. "Hey, Priscilla," she hissed. She waved Priscilla's pencil case and snickered.

*   *   *

"How was your second day of school?" asked Priscilla's father that night at dinner.

"Terrible!" said Priscilla.

"Rrrrgrr," barked Pow-wow from under the dinner table.

"Did you make new friends?" asked Priscilla's mother.

Priscilla stuck her fork prongs into the tablecloth. "Felicity Doll wants to be my friend."

"That's nice," said Priscilla's mother. She passed Priscilla a plate of beef stew. "I am glad you two girls made up."

"Pris-cil-la," said Eve. "May I see you for a moment in the kitchen?"

Priscilla followed Eve through the swinging door. Pow-wow followed Priscilla.

Eve shook her head. "You've been at school two days, Priscilla, and you've already made a giant mistake."

"Making friends with Felicity?" guessed Priscilla.

"Felicity does not know how to be a friend," said

Eve. "Felicity knows how to be a snake.

"Rrrrgrr," barked Pow-wow.

Priscilla nodded. "Yesterday Felicity stole my desk. Today she took my pencil case."

"You need someone to stick up for you," said Eve. "Do you want me to make Felicity give your things back?"

Priscilla wanted her things back. "But," she thought, "Felicity will trap me again with another one of her tricks. . . ."

"Eve?" called their mother from the dining room. "Priscilla? Dinner is getting cold!"

"Thank you," Priscilla told Eve. "But I think I'd better stick up for myself."

The next morning Felicity wanted to trade lunch boxes.

"I have a lunch box," said Priscilla. "You carry your lunch in a paper bag."

"Friends share." Felicity smiled her snakey smile.

Before Priscilla knew what happened, Felicity

carried off Priscilla's lunch box. Felicity put the lunch box inside the beautiful desk that should have been Priscilla's. She put it right next to the brand-new pencil case that Priscilla could only see from a distance.

At lunch Felicity spilled tomato juice on her pink sweater.

"Friends share," Felicity told Priscilla. Before Priscilla knew it, Felicity had taken Priscilla's soft yellow sweater.

"What will I do with this?" Priscilla wrinkled her nose. Felicity had left her the soggy pink mess.

"Felicity Doll has gone too far!" Eve said to Priscilla after dinner that night. "She took your pencil case, and your lunch box, and now your sweater—"

"Don't forget my desk," said Priscilla.

"She cannot push around my little sister!" Eve made a fist. "Tomorrow—"

"Eve," said Priscilla, "let me try one last time."

The next morning Priscilla arrived at school. Felicity waited beside her desk.

"I did not do my homework," said Felicity. "Lend me your paper. I will copy the answers."

Priscilla opened her mouth to say "NO!"

"Well?" said Felicity.

Priscilla shut her mouth. She had an idea. "Here is my homework." She handed Felicity her paper. She smiled a Felicity smile.

"Friends share," she said.

Felicity looked at the paper. She looked hard at Priscilla. "Is there something wrong with this homework—?"

Brnnnggg! The bell rang.

"Settle down, class." Ms. Cobble clapped her hands.

Felicity snatched Priscilla's paper and hurried to her seat.

Priscilla watched Felicity take off *her* soft yellow sweater. She watched Felicity hang it over the back

23

of *her* chair. She watched Felicity take a brand-new pencil out of *her* pencil case. Felicity began to copy *her* homework—

"Ms. Cobble!" Priscilla raised her hand. She waved it.

Ms. Cobble turned from the blackboard. "Priscilla, whatever is the trouble?"

Priscilla took a deep breath. "Felicity Doll is sitting at my desk."

Ms. Cobble looked at Felicity. She looked at Priscilla. "We already settled this matter, Priscilla."

"Ask Felicity whose lunch box is in that desk," said Priscilla.

"Felicity?" said Ms. Cobble.

"Wel-l-l-l," said Felicity.

"Ask her whose pencil case is in that desk," said Priscilla.

Ms. Cobble looked stern.

"Uhnnn—" said Felicity.

"That is my yellow sweater hanging over the back of Felicity's chair," said Priscilla.

———

Ms. Cobble frowned.

Felicity looked at her feet.

"That is my homework on top of the desk," said Priscilla.

"Fe-li-city!" said Ms. Cobble. "Is this true?"

Felicity's voice sounded squeaky. "Yes."

"Priscilla," said Ms. Cobble. "Felicity, I think you had better change desks."

"I'll get you," hissed Felicity as she passed Priscilla.

Priscilla sat down at the beautiful desk. "I doubt it," she thought.

"How was school today?" asked Priscilla's father that night at dinner.

"Rrrruf," yipped Pow-wow.

"Excellent," said Priscilla.

Priscilla's mother asked, "Did you play with your friend, Felicity Doll?"

"Felicity Doll is no longer my friend," said Priscilla. "Please pass the brussels sprouts."

"Not your friend?" Priscilla's mother looked concerned. "Whatever happened?"

Eve choked on her macaroni. "Yes, Priscilla, tell us what happened."

Pow-wow yawned. "Eeeehh."

Priscilla took a sip of milk. She smoothed the sleeves of her soft yellow sweater. "After school today, Felicity stopped me. She told me that we are no longer friends. 'We are enemies!' she said."

Priscilla's mother sighed.

Priscilla's father shook his head.

"Felicity has a new best friend," said Priscilla. "Her name is Lucille Bingay."

"How sad!" said Eve, but she was giggling. "You must feel just awful."

Priscilla speared a brussels sprout. "I don't feel nearly as awful as poor Lucille."

2. Ugly Shoes

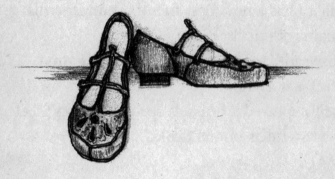

That Saturday afternoon Priscilla's mother drove Priscilla downtown. Pow-wow sat in the backseat with his nose out the window. He waited in the car while they went into Tipton's Shoe Store.

"You may choose any shoes at all," said Priscilla's mother. "But pick a pair you really like. These shoes must last you the whole school year."

Priscilla looked at the shoes in the store window. She saw a pair just like the ones she was wearing. Brown, with laces. She looked at the shoes lined up on a shelf in the store. She saw a fancy pair. "Just like the shoes Felicity Doll wears every day," thought Priscilla. The shoes were white patent leather with bows and flowers.

Priscilla looked at the shoes that stood on the table in front of the trying-on chairs. She saw just the shoes she wanted.

They were dark red. They had pinhole designs swirling over the toes. Instead of laces that would always get stuck in knots, these shoes had straps.

"May I try those?" said Priscilla. While Priscilla sat in a trying-on chair, Mr. Tipton pulled a box from a shelf and opened it up.

Priscilla slid her feet into the beautiful shoes. She buckled the straps. She walked up and down the store. In front of the mirror she stopped. The beautiful shoes gleamed. "These are the ones I want."

Priscilla's mother examined the shoes. "Do your feet have enough room to grow?" She pressed the toes. "They are a perfect fit. Are you sure you will like these shoes, day after day?"

Priscilla said, "I am sure."

"They are lovely shoes," agreed Mr. Tipton. He put the shoes in their box. He put the box in a bag and handed it to Priscilla.

On Monday morning Priscilla wore her new shoes to school. The dark red leather shone. The small gold buckles gleamed. The pinhole designs swirled. Priscilla opened her classroom door. She stepped inside—

"Hey!" There stood Felicity. Felicity Doll wore one of her ruffly dresses, as usual. She wore the white patent leather shoes with the bows and flowers, and socks with ruffles made of lace.

"What do you call those things?" Felicity pointed.

"I call them my new shoes," said Priscilla. "I picked them myself."

"You picked those?" said Felicity. She squatted down to take a closer look. Priscilla looked, too.

The pinhole designs swirled over her toes. The straps lay snugly buckled. The dark red leather gleamed.

Felicity straightened up. "I've got news for you," she said. "Those are the ugliest shoes I have ever seen."

Felicity fluffed her curly hair. She looked at Priscilla's shoes. "Ug-ly!" And off she flounced.

Priscilla's feet turned to stone. Her cheeks burned. She stared at the beautiful shoes she had picked out herself. They looked gigantic. They looked ugly.

Brrnnngg! The bell rang.

Priscilla hurried to her chair. She jammed her feet into the dark under her desk.

"Settle down, class," clapped Ms. Cobble. "Roger, it is your turn to begin the morning as our

———

Show-and-Tell person. Lucille, tomorrow is your turn. Priscilla, Wednesday will be your Show-and-Tell day."

Roger stood. "This is the model jet plane I built on Saturday. . . ."

At her desk in the front row, Felicity turned. "Pssst," she hissed at Priscilla. She pointed to the darkness under Priscilla's desk. She held her nose and made a face. She mouthed one word, "Ug-ly!"

On Tuesday morning Priscilla dressed. She stepped into her blue corduroy pants. She pulled her maroon sweater over her head. She yanked on one blue-and-maroon striped sock and then the other. She stuck her feet into her shoes. The old brown shoes with the laces.

"Where are your snazzy new shoes?" asked her father when Priscilla sat down for breakfast.

"I am saving those shoes for special occasions," said Priscilla. "I do not want to wear them out."

Priscilla's mother passed the toast. "I am glad you are being careful with your new shoes. But you needn't worry about wearing them out. They are meant to be worn every day."

Eve gave Priscilla a long look. "I'll bet I know

why Priscilla isn't wearing her new shoes—"

"Catch!" Priscilla tossed Pow-wow a piece of toast.

"Wrrruf!" barked Pow-wow.

"Priscilla!" scolded her mother. "No feeding Pow-wow from the table."

"Sorry," said Priscilla.

"Eat up, then," said her father. Both her parents went back to reading the newspaper. Over the breakfast table Eve was still giving Priscilla that searching look.

"I must go," said Priscilla. "Or I will be late for school." She put down her spoon and left.

For Show-and-Tell, Lucille presented the postcard her aunt had sent from Europe. She pointed to the back. "The stamps have weird lions on them."

At recess Felicity was waiting for Priscilla at the classroom door. She said, "Where are those ugly shoes?"

"I do not know what you are talking about," said Priscilla.

"Yes you do," Felicity said. She smiled her snakey smile. She twirled a curl of hair around her finger. "Sometime you will have to wear those new shoes again." She made a face and held her nose. "Ug-ly!"

"Priscilla!" At breakfast on Wednesday morning Priscilla's mother said, "March right back to your room. Take off those old brown shoes and put on your new red ones."

"I do not want to wear those shoes," said Priscilla. "Those shoes are ugly."

"Wrrooouu," howled Pow-wow.

"Those shoes were quite expensive," said Priscilla's mother.

"Who called them ugly?" said Priscilla's father.

"Just as I thought," Eve nodded wisely. "Felicity Doll made fun of them."

"She did more than that," sighed Priscilla. "She

said they were the ugliest shoes she had ever seen."

"That Felicity!" Priscilla's father stirred his coffee so hard, it splashed onto his saucer.

"Felicity Doll is just jealous." Priscilla's mother patted Priscilla on the head. "Your new shoes are perfectly beautiful. You scoot right back to your room and put them on."

"If I must change my shoes, I will change my pants, too," Priscilla told Pow-wow. She put on her brown pants, the ones with the extra-long legs. As she climbed the school steps Priscilla watched her feet. "Good," she thought. "I can barely see my new shoes." Priscilla opened the classroom door—

"Ha!" Felicity jumped out at her. "I see you are wearing those ugly shoes again. Look!" She said to Lucille Bingay. "Look at the shoes Priscilla picked out herself. Aren't they the ugliest shoes you have ever seen?"

Brrnnngg! The bell rang.

Priscilla hurried to her desk. She jammed her

feet into the dark under her desk.

"Settle down, class," clapped Ms. Cobble. "Priscilla, it is your turn to start us off with Show-and-Tell."

Priscilla froze. She thought, "I forgot all about Show-and-Tell."

"Come to the front of the room," said Ms. Cobble.

Priscilla struggled from her chair. Slowly, slowly she made her way to the front of the room.

"You may stand right here in front of Felicity's desk." Although Ms. Cobble changed class seating each month, Felicity always wound up seated front and center.

Priscilla looked at Felicity.

Felicity smiled up at her with her snakey smile. Her eyes narrowed in a *now-I've-got-you* smirk.

"Well, Priscilla?" said Ms. Cobble.

Priscilla had nothing to show.

Ms. Cobble said, "What are you going to tell us about today?" The whole class was staring at Priscilla and waiting.

Priscilla said, "I have new shoes."

She rolled up her pants legs so that everyone could see the dark red shoes. "I picked them myself."

Felicity raised her hand. She waved it. "Ms. Cobble, I think Priscilla's shoes are—"

"Not now, Felicity," said Ms. Cobble. "Priscilla, may I take a closer look at those shoes?"

The whole class leaned forward as Ms. Cobble stooped to inspect Priscilla's new shoes.

"I once had a pair of shoes just like these," said Ms. Cobble.

"You did?" said the class.

"They were dark red leather, with straps that buckled and a design that swirled over the toes. . . ."

"Ooooohhhh," said the class.

Ms. Cobble straightened up. "Priscilla," she said. "Thank you for sharing your new shoes with us. They are perfectly beautiful."

"Beautiful," the class agreed. They all leaned back in their seats.

"Now, Felicity," said Ms. Cobble. "What did you want to say?"

Felicity looked hard at Priscilla. Priscilla looked hard right back.

"I forget," said Felicity. She slumped down deep into her chair.

Priscilla skipped back to her desk. Her red shoes shone, the buckles gleamed, and the pinhole designs swirled.

"You can tell us when you remember," said Ms. Cobble.

"I will," mumbled Felicity.

But Priscilla knew that she wouldn't.

3. Good Sport, Bad Sport

Priscilla's school had Sports Day twice each year, once in the fall and once in the spring. Each Sports Day, Eve ran in the Girls' Sprint for her grade.

On Fall Sports Day, Eve won the sprint by a full second. Mr. Wentzle, the gym teacher, told Priscilla, "Eve trained well. She runs faster than any girl in her grade."

On Spring Sports Day, Eve won the sprint by two seconds. Eve's boyfriend D.J. told Priscilla, "Eve practiced every day. She runs faster than any girl in the school." D.J. and Priscilla watched Mr. Wentzle pin the blue ribbon onto Eve's running shirt.

"Hooray!" cheered everyone in the school.

Eve blushed. Priscilla felt proud.

"Awesome," said D.J. He looked as though he would like to kiss Eve. "There is no faster runner in this town than your sister," he said.

"I would not bet on that," said a familiar voice.

"Oh no," thought Priscilla. She turned to look. Felicity Doll stood beside her.

Felicity wore ruffled shorts. She wore a ruffled blouse. Even Felicity's socks had ruffles.

"Eve is not so great," she said. She batted her eyelashes at D.J. "My sister Nanette would have won that race if Mr. Wentzle had not disqualified her for shoving."

"Baloney!" said D.J.

"You wish!" said Priscilla.

Felicity fluffed her ruffles. She stuck her nose in the air. "Wait until Fall Sports Day. I plan to enter the Girls' Sprint for our grade. And—" she stuck her tongue out at Priscilla, "I plan to win." Away she flounced.

Priscilla had plans, too.

All summer long Priscilla dreamed of running in the Girls' Sprint. She dreamed of charging across the starting line the way Eve did. She dreamed of racing down the cinder track as fast as the wind. She dreamed of crossing the finish line in a final burst of speed. She dreamed that Mr. Wentzle pinned a blue ribbon onto her running shirt while everyone in the school cheered. D.J. and Eve cheered the most. Felicity was nowhere to be seen.

Priscilla did more than dream. She practiced just as Eve did. Pow-wow practiced with her.

Each morning Priscilla sprinted up one side of

their street and down the other.

Each afternoon she rode her bike down the big hill to the park. There she ran once around the duck pond. She stretched. She rested. She gulped water from the fountain. She ran around the pond once more. Pow-wow ran alongside.

"Hehh-hehh-hehh," Priscilla panted as she rode her bike up the big hill toward home.

Pow-wow ran beside her and panted, too.

"You are wasting your time," a familiar voice called.

"Rrrggrr," growled Pow-wow.

"Oh no," said Priscilla.

Felicity Doll lounged in a hammock on her porch. She licked an ice cream cone. "Give up!" shouted Felicity. "I am the fastest thing on two feet. Come Fall Sports Day, that blue ribbon will belong to me!" A glob of ice cream melted off the cone and fell on Felicity's ruffled bathing suit.

"Come on, Pow-wow," said Priscilla. She pedaled harder than ever. She topped the hill and coasted

down the other side. "Who cares what that show–off thinks?" she said, but she knew the answer. She cared. Priscilla was worried.

★   ★   ★

"Felicity says she can run like the wind," Priscilla told Eve before dinner that evening.

Eve was doing warm-up exercises. "Have you seen Felicity run?" asked Eve.

"Yes," said Priscilla. "Mr. Wentzle made her run twice a week in gym class."

Eve pulled up her socks. "Is she fast?"

Priscilla thought about Felicity huffing up the cinder track. She thought of Felicity turning and puffing down the track. "Felicity Doll is just about the pokiest runner I have ever seen," said Priscilla. "I think all those ruffles slow her down."

Eve ran in place. "If Felicity is so slow, why are you worried?"

"It is hard to explain," said Priscilla. "Felicity is slow, but Felicity wants that blue ribbon. What Felicity wants, Felicity is tricky enough to get."

"You are right," said Eve. "Felicity Doll is a real snake."

———

Summer vacation ended. School started. Priscilla and Felicity were both in Ms. Tweet's second grade.

One week before Fall Sports Day, Ms. Tweet assigned everyone to a Sports Day event. "Let's have volunteers for the Three-legged Race," she said.

Priscilla kept her hand in her lap.

So did Felicity.

Ms. Tweet chose Heidi and Jill as one team. She chose Stan and Butch as another. "Who would like to be in the Broad Jump?" said Ms. Tweet.

Priscilla did not raise her hand. Neither did Felicity.

Ms. Tweet chose Dex, William, Josie, and Evelyn. Ms. Tweet chose competitors for the High Jump, the Relays, and the Boys' Sprint. "I think that takes care of everything," said Ms. Tweet.

"No!" cried Priscilla. Everyone turned to look at her. "You forgot the Girls' Sprint," she said.

"So I did," said Ms. Tweet. "Any volunteers, class?"

Felicity shot her hand high. She waved it in front of Ms. Tweet. "Me-me-me-me-me!" whined Felicity.

Ms. Tweet laughed. "You have your heart set on this event, Felicity. You must be a fast runner."

"Yes," said Felicity. "I run faster than anyone you've ever seen."

"What a snake!" thought Priscilla.

Ms. Tweet smiled. "You may run in the Girls' Sprint," she said. "Any other volunteers?" she looked around the classroom.

Priscilla held her hand straight up in the air. Her arm ached from holding it so high.

"Meg," said Ms. Tweet. "You may run in the Sprint, too."

Priscilla raised her hand still higher. She whispered, "Please, pick me."

Felicity gave Priscilla a snakey smile. "Ms. Tweet!" she called in a syrupy voice. "You've already picked Meg and me, and each class may enter only two runners."

Ms. Tweet looked puzzled. "Thank you for telling me that rule," she said. "I had not heard it."

"Oh no!" thought Priscilla. She raised her hand higher still. She waved it.

Finally Ms. Tweet looked Priscilla's way. She turned to Felicity, "If there is such a rule, I will ask Mr. Wentzle to make one exception. Priscilla reminded us of the Sprint. She deserves to race, too."

"Wheww," thought Priscilla. She lowered her hand.

Felicity turned to her and glared. She held up her index finger. She pointed to herself. "I am Number One!" she mouthed.

"We will see about that," thought Priscilla, but she did not feel sure.

Each day during recess everyone practiced. On Monday, Priscilla did warm-up exercises beside the cinder track. Felicity stood and watched. "I am going to leave you in the dust," Felicity told Priscilla.

"That's what you say," said Priscilla. She ran as

fast as she could down the track. "Let's see you do that," she yelled at Felicity. Felicity fluffed her ruffles. "When you are as fast a runner as I am, you don't need to practice," she said. Off she flounced.

"Maybe she is a faster runner than I know," Priscilla could not help thinking.

On Tuesday, Felicity carried a shoe box onto the playground. She opened the box to show Priscilla what was inside.

Brand-new running shoes. They were pink with silver laces and silver wings on the sides. "My dad bought them for me," said Felicity. "When I wear them, I run like the wind." She put the top back on the shoe box. "Too bad you don't have new running shoes," she said.

Priscilla looked at her old blue sneakers.

"You don't stand a chance in those things," said Felicity.

"Maybe she is right," thought Priscilla.

★　　★　　★

On Wednesday, Felicity carried a fancy paper bag to the playground. She opened the bag to show Priscilla what was inside.

Brand-new running shorts and a brand-new running shirt. They were lavender with silver lightning bolts on them and silver ruffles. "My mom bought them for me," said Felicity. "I look like a champion when I wear them. I am saving them for Sports Day."

Felicity poked Priscilla in the chest. "You might as well stay home. You haven't got a chance." She closed her fancy bag. Away she flounced.

"Felicity is right," thought Priscilla. "She is going to beat me."

Thursday after school, Priscilla told Eve and D.J. the whole story. "Felicity has new running shoes. She has new running shorts and a running shirt with bolts of lightning on them. Felicity can run so fast, she does not need to practice—"

"Baloney!" said D.J.

"Rrrggrr," growled Pow-wow.

"That Felicity!" Eve tied her running shoes. She pulled on her duckbill cap. She ran in place. "Felicity Doll is trying to scare you."

"Trying?" Priscilla said. "Felicity has me terrified."

Eve stopped running. She took Priscilla by the shoulders and looked straight into Priscilla's eyes. "Don't let Felicity fool you."

D.J. said, "Keep practicing."

Eve let go of Priscilla's shoulders. She ran in place again. "For a little kid, you are pretty fast." Eve turned to run down the driveway. "I'll bet you win that race."

D.J. took off after Eve. "Remember," he called to Priscilla, "we'll be rooting for you!"

Priscilla looked at Pow-wow. "I am pretty fast for a little kid," she told him. "Felicity Doll will need more than fancy clothes to beat me."

"Rrrggrr!" growled Pow-wow.

★   ★   ★

On Friday morning Priscilla sat down to breakfast. "All set for the big race?" asked her father.

"Did you get a good night's sleep?" asked her mother.

Priscilla wiggled her toes in her old blue sneakers. "I slept well," said Priscilla. She wiped her sweaty palms on her shorts. "I am all set."

Eve winked at Priscilla. She made a fist with just her thumb sticking up. "I have a good feeling about this race," said Eve. "I bet Priscilla wins."

Priscilla ate her cereal. "No, thank you," she said when her father offered her bacon. "Too much cholesterol slows a person down." Priscilla put on her sweater. She picked up her lunch box. She kissed her father and mother goodbye. She waved to Powwow and Eve. "Here goes," she said.

"Prepare to be blown away," said Felicity. She stood next to Priscilla on the starting line. Felicity wore the pink running shoes with the silver laces and silver wings. She wore the lavender shorts with the silver lightning bolts and ruffles and the matching top.

"On your marks—" said Mr. Wentzle.

"Here comes the Human Rocket," said Felicity.

"Get set—" said Mr. Wentzle. He shot the starter's gun. "Go!"

Priscilla felt Felicity charge across the starting line. Priscilla charged across, too.

Pound—pound—pound—

Priscilla kept her eyes focused on the white chalk finish line.

Pound—pound—pound—

She ran with all her might.

Pound—pound—pound—

She reached the finish line. She crossed it.

Pound—pound—pound—

Priscilla was running so fast she could not stop.

Pound—pound—pound—

"Whewww!" Then she could.

"Yea!" shouted the spectators. "Yea!"

———

Priscilla looked about her. All the other runners were trying to catch their breath, too. The girls from Ms. Kneff's class collapsed on the ground by the finish line.

Priscilla wondered, "Who won?"

"I'll bet I broke the school record," said a familiar voice.

"Oh no," thought Priscilla. She turned to look. Felicity stood beside her.

Felicity's face was red and sweaty. She did not look like someone who had just won a sprint. Felicity said, "Here comes Mr. Wentzle. That is my blue ribbon he is carrying."

Priscilla looked.

Mr. Wentzle stepped onto the track. He carried a yellow ribbon, a red ribbon, and a blue one.

Priscilla stood still.

Priscilla's heart raced.

Mr. Wentzle stopped beside Meg. He handed her the yellow ribbon.

Mr. Wentzle walked by the runners from Ms.

Kneff's class. He stopped before one of the girls from Mr. Wrigley's class. He handed the red ribbon to her.

"At last," said Felicity. "The moment I have been waiting for."

Mr. Wentzle crossed the track. He stopped in front of Priscilla and Felicity.

Pound—pound—pound—

"I award this ribbon to the fastest girl in the second grade," announced Mr. Wentzle. "Priscilla Robin!"

"Hooraay!" Everyone in the school cheered.

"Hooraay!" Eve, D.J., and Priscilla's mother and father cheered, too. "Hooraay!"

Only one person did not cheer. "I have been robbed," muttered Felicity.

Priscilla wore her blue ribbon all the rest of the school day. At 2:30 Ms. Tweet spoke to the class. "I am proud of each one of you." She smiled at

Priscilla, Meg, and Dex. "I am proud of those of you who won ribbons." Ms. Tweet smiled at Felicity. "I am proud of those of you who tried."

Josie giggled.

Butch snickered.

Felicity scowled. Felicity had not placed first. She had not placed second or third. She had not received

an honorable mention. Felicity Doll, the Human Rocket, had finished last.

Brrnnngg! The final bell rang.

"Class dismissed!" said Ms. Tweet.

Priscilla put on her sweater. She picked up her lunch box and walked out the school door.

Felicity stood waiting for her.

"I could have beaten you," said Felicity.

"You don't say?" said Priscilla.

Felicity pointed. "These new shoes pinched my feet. My knee hurt. I had a dizzy spell."

"I am sorry to hear that," said Priscilla. "You should go home and lie down." She stepped past Felicity. "Goodbye."

"Hey!" Felicity ran ahead. She stood in Priscilla's path. She jabbed Priscilla in the chest. "Just wait until Spring Sports Day," she said. Felicity glared at Priscilla's blue ribbon.

A breeze lifted the ribbon. It fluttered cheerfully against Priscilla's blouse.

———

"You cannot wear that ribbon to school tomorrow," said Felicity. "You will be in big trouble if you do." She gave Priscilla the nasty look that always made her feel nervous.

"You're right," said Priscilla. She touched the ribbon. "I can wear this ribbon only today."

Felicity smiled her meanest smile. She fluffed her ruffles.

But it didn't make Priscilla nervous. "Felicity," she said in a friendly way. "Do you know when *you* will get to wear a blue ribbon?"

Felicity's mouth dropped open. "When?" she asked.

"Never!" shouted Priscilla.

Felicity's face turned red. She stamped her foot. She shook her fist. "You show-off!" cried Felicity.

But the fastest girl in the second grade had already sprinted out of sight.

———

4. The Birthday

October twelfth was Priscilla's birthday. This year it fell on a Saturday.

"You may invite twelve friends," said Priscilla's mother. "We will drive to Lockhart's Farm."

"Lockhart's Farm!" cried Priscilla.

"Wroou-wroou." Pow-wow chased his tail.

Lockhart's Farm was Priscilla's favorite place. The

---

farm had goats that people could feed. It had pigs and sheep and chickens. A red rooster strutted in the barnyard. Six ponies cantered around the paddock. Next to the paddock was a pond with paddleboats in it. Inside the big white barn a machine pressed apples into cider. Behind the barn, fields of flowers and vegetables spread up a hill. In the largest patch, orange pumpkins grew.

The Lockharts sold their produce at a garden stand beside the road. People drove their cars into the parking lot. They bought apples, cider, Indian corn, zinnias, and pumpkins for Halloween. Next door stood the Jack O'Lantern Restaurant. It had long wooden tables with tree stumps for seats. Sawdust covered the floor. The giant hearth was filled with balloons. Behind the grill, Mr. Lockhart stood and cooked hamburgers. Mrs. Lockhart baked in the kitchen. Jack and Janice Lockhart took orders and served food.

When someone had a birthday at the Jack O'Lantern, Mrs. Lockhart baked a special cake. She wrote "Happy Birthday" and the person's name in colored icing around the top. At the cake's very center, she placed a miniature farm animal made of glass. Sometimes the animal was a cow. Sometimes, a rooster or a sheep. The birthday person got to keep the animal as a souvenir. "I hope Mrs. Lockhart puts a pony on my cake," Priscilla told her mother. Ponies were Priscilla's favorite.

"We will drive to the farm on Saturday morning," said Priscilla's father. "You and your guests will have time to take a paddleboat ride and feed the animals before lunch. Afterward, everyone may choose a small pumpkin to take home."

"This will be the best birthday party anyone ever had," Priscilla told Eve the next afternoon. It was Saturday. Priscilla's birthday was one week away. She and Eve walked to the corner mailbox so that Priscilla could mail her party invitations.

"Wroou-wroou." Pow-wow ran ahead.

"Did you invite Heidi?" asked Eve.

"Here is Heidi's invitation," said Priscilla.

"What about Butch and Stan and Evelyn?"

Priscilla showed Eve the stamped envelopes. "I have written invitations to all of them."

Pow-wow reached the mailbox. "Arrrouuu," he yawned. He waited for them to catch up.

Eve asked, "Did you remember Jill and Dennis?"

"Of course," said Priscilla. "Also Dex." They reached the mailbox. Priscilla pulled down the handle. She placed the invitations inside—

"Wait," said Eve. "What about Felicity? Did you invite Felicity Doll?"

Priscilla let go the handle. *Bangg!* The mailbox slammed shut.

"This is a party for friends," said Priscilla. "No snakes allowed!"

"Rrrggrr," Pow-wow agreed.

Eve thought for a moment. Slowly she shook her head. "Felicity will hear about this party. She will be furious."

★   ★   ★

On Tuesday morning Felicity met Priscilla at the classroom door. "I hope you have a birthday party invitation for me." She stared at Priscilla in the way that always made her feel nervous.

Priscilla did not want to listen to nasty remarks. She said, "Get out of my way, please."

Felicity did not budge. "You did not invite me to your party. You invited Jill and Stan and Dennis—"

Priscilla studied the toes of her shoes. Felicity spoke in a voice that was soft and snakey.

"—you invited Evelyn and Heidi and Butch—"

Priscilla shifted her lunch box from her right hand to her left.

"—you invited *everybody* but me."

Priscilla cleared her throat. She looked up. "My mother said I could ask twelve friends. We are not friends, Felicity. You do nasty things to me."

A tear coasted down Felicity's cheek. She wiped it away. "I have been mean to you, Priscilla. I don't blame you for leaving me out." She turned and plodded to her desk.

Priscilla's birthday excitement vanished. "Felicity feels awful because of my party." She hung her head.

Priscilla's father supposed that one more party guest would be all right.

"Here is another invitation," said Priscilla's mother. "Go ahead and address it."

Carefully, Priscilla printed on the small white envelope, "F-E-L-I-C-I-T-Y—"

"Rrrggrr," growled Pow-wow.

Eve said, "Are you sure you want to do this?"

"—D-O-L-L." Priscilla lifted her pencil. She felt better. "I'm sure."

Priscilla's mother glued the postage stamp to the envelope. "Felicity Doll makes a baker's dozen for your party."

Eve looked grim. "That is a nice way of saying Felicity makes Unlucky Thirteen."

COME AT 10 A.M.

said Priscilla's party invitations

WEAR PLAY CLOTHES

Bonggg-bonggg. At 9:30 on Saturday morning the Robins' doorbell rang. *Bonggg-bonggg. Bonggg-bonggg. Bonggg-bonggg.*

Priscilla's mother switched off the vacuum cleaner. "Who can that be?"

"Maybe it's D.J." said Eve.

"Maybe it's the mailman with a birthday card for me," said Priscilla.

"Rroughhh-wrroo," barked Pow-wow.

They all hurried to the front hall. Priscilla's mother opened the door. "Why, Felicity has come early."

"Wouldn't you know it," whispered Eve.

Felicity was not wearing jeans, or overalls, or sweatpants. "Good morning, Mrs. Robin." Felicity smoothed the ruffles of her fancy lavender party dress. She smiled so that a dimple creased each cheek. "I could not wait a minute longer to say Happy Birthday to my best friend Pixi!"

"Pixi?" said Priscilla's mother.

"Pixi?" said Eve.

Priscilla's stomach felt funny.

"Priscilla invited me to this party because she felt sorry for me." Felicity's dimples deepened. "I am grateful. I have played my last dirty trick on Priscilla. Starting now, I will be her best friend."

———

Priscilla nudged Eve. "I have heard *that* line before."

"I have not had much practice being a friend," admitted Felicity. She fluffed her ruffles. "But how difficult can it be? Heidi and Evelyn are best friends. I studied them all week. I know just how to act. Rule number one: friends give each other pet names."

"Tough luck." Eve patted Priscilla's shoulder. "In the past Felicity pretended to be your friend. This time she means it, Pixi."

"You do not need to do a thing," Felicity told Priscilla. "I have this friendship business all figured out."

The doorbell rang. Jill arrived, then Stan.

"Relax," Felicity went on. "Leave everything to me."

Priscilla did not know what else she could do. "I guess we can give it a try."

By ten past ten all the guests had arrived. Priscilla's

father backed his car out of the garage. "Half you girls and boys hop into Mr. Robin's car," Priscilla's mother said. "The other half go with Priscilla's Aunt Jean."

"Watch this." Felicity nudged Priscilla. "I have this best-friend routine down cold." Suddenly, Felicity squinched her face and squealed, "Pixi-Pixi-Pixi-Pixi! I get to sit next to Pixi!" Before Priscilla could stop her, Felicity grabbed her hand. *Smack—Smack—Smack,* she kissed it—

"Stop!" Priscilla yanked away her hand. "Stop!" She hid it behind her back.

"I will stop only if you let me sit next to you." Felicity smiled her dimply smile.

Priscilla was too tired to argue. She climbed into the car. "Get in," she said.

Felicity did not budge. She fluffed her ruffles. "Call me by my pet name. Call me Fels."

Priscilla sighed. "Very well, Fels. Get in!"

★ ★ ★

The cars arrived at Lockhart's Farm. All the guests jumped out. "Everyone who wants a paddleboat ride, head over to the wading pond and put on a life preserver," said Mrs. Lockhart.

Each paddleboat was big enough for two people.

"Hey, Priscilla," said Butch. "Want to ride with me?"

Priscilla's fingers tingled. Her skin felt warm.

"Push off, Butch," Felicity grabbed Priscilla's arm. "Pixi is paddleboating with me!"

"Fe-*li*-city!" Priscilla pulled her aside. "I *want* to paddleboat with Butch. He is my boyfriend."

"*Boy*friend?" shrieked Felicity.

Butch glared. Jill and Dennis giggled. Stan covered his mouth and snickered.

"*Boy*friend?" Felicity shrieked again. "Who cares about a *boy*friend? You have a *best* friend, me!"

Priscilla paddleboated with Felicity.

"Isn't this fun?" Felicity beamed.

Butch and Jill paddled by in another boat. They

were laughing. Priscilla frowned. "It would be more fun if you did some of the paddling, Felicity."

"Time to feed the animals!" called Mr. Lockhart.

All the guests pulled their boats ashore. They ran up the hills to the barnyard. "Time to feed the animals!" Priscilla ran, too. As she ran, she pulled from her pocket the carrot for her favorite pony, Whizbang.

She reached Whizbang's paddock. She climbed the fence. She stretched her arm—

"Look out, Pixi!" Felicity snatched the carrot. "Ponies sometimes bite."

She offered Whizbang Priscilla's carrot.

Whizbang gently nibbled it. "Neeiihh," he whinnied once, then cantered away.

Felicity looked at her fingers. "Ickkk, pony drool." She wiped her hand on the fence. Then she flung her arm around Priscilla's shoulders. "What fun thing shall we do next?"

At lunch Priscilla sat between Eve and Dex. She munched her hamburger. She sipped her cider. "I am glad Felicity is seated at the other end of the table," she told Eve. "Even a best friend needs a rest from Felicity."

"Excuse me—" a familiar voice insisted.

Priscilla saw Felicity pushing her way toward her. Felicity elbowed aside Dex. "Excuse me. I have something private to tell Pixi." She placed her left hand on Priscilla's shoulder. She leaned close to whisper in Priscilla's ear—

"Look out!" yelled Dex.

Felicity's right hand banged Priscilla's glass. *Crashh!* Cider spilled all over Priscilla's jeans.

"Pixi!" Felicity grabbed Priscilla's paper napkin. She dabbed at Priscilla's wet jeans. She turned to Dex. "I hope you are happy with the mess you have made! Boys are so rowdy."

Jack Lockhart cleared away the hamburger plates. Janice Lockhart helped Priscilla sponge off her jeans.

Felicity returned to her seat at the table's far end.

"This is not exactly the birthday party I had in mind," Priscilla told Eve.

"Cheer up," said Eve. "After the cake, even your best friend will go home."

The cake. Priscilla had nearly forgotten. What glass animal would she find on top? A sheep? A rooster? "Please let it be a pony." She crossed her fingers.

"Happy Birthday to you—" Mrs. Lockhart stepped through the kitchen door. Candles flickered. She was carrying Priscilla's birthday cake. "Happy Birthday to you—" sang everyone.

"Chocolate frosting!" cried Dex.

"Roses!" Evelyn bounced on her tree stump. "Pink ones!"

Felicity eyed the icing flowers. "They are not as big as they ought to be, but they will have to do."

Priscilla did not notice the pink roses. She did not notice the chocolate icing. She forgot how soggy her blue jeans felt. Inside the shining circle of candles on top of her birthday cake pranced a miniature glass horse.

Mrs. Lockhart placed the cake in front of Priscilla. "Make a wish, dear. Blow out the candles."

"I already have my wish," said Priscilla. She pointed to the pony. "That is it."

"I have a wish!" shrieked Felicity. "Let me make a wish on your cake, Pixi. Let me do it! Please-please-please?"

Priscilla did not know what to say.

"Pleeeeeze?"

"Okay," shrugged Priscilla.

"Oboy-oboy-oboy-oboy." Felicity rushed to stand beside Priscilla. "I wish—" Felicity clasped her hands and closed her eyes. "—that Priscilla and I will be as good friends forever as we are today."

"Look out!" yelled Dex.

"Ohhhnooo!" cried Eve.

Whhssssss, Felicity huffed. Every candle on Priscilla's cake blew out.

———

"That does it!" cried Priscilla.

"Stop gabbing," called Stan. "Cut the cake!"

"Cut the cake!" chanted everyone. "Cut the cake!"

At the center of the cake, the little pony sparkled. "I got my wish," thought Priscilla. She forgot about being angry at Felicity. She picked up the cake cutter. "Uhfff." She needed both hands to hold it; it was heavy. "I do not think I can manage. This cutter is too big—"

"I will help!" Felicity raced back to Priscilla's side.

Priscilla clutched the cake cutter. "No!"

Felicity grabbed. "I am an expert cake slicer. I will slice this cake so that you get not one rose, but two!"

"Fe-*li*-city!" Priscilla wrestled the cake cutter toward her.

"*Pix*-i!" Felicity wrestled it right back.

Priscilla pulled. "I do not need your help—"

Felicity yanked—

Spluttt! The cake cutter smashed flat onto the top of the cake. *Crkk!* Priscilla's glass pony disappeared.

"My dress!" shrieked Felicity. Chocolate frosting

spattered her lavender ruffles. Pink icing hung in her hair. "You have ruined my dress!" She glared at Priscilla. "You have spoiled my Saturday! This friendship business is for the birds." She wiped icing from her nose and stalked off. "Consider us enemies!"

"My pony!" whispered Priscilla.

"Relax." Eve searched the center of the smashed cake with her fork. Priscilla saw something sparkle. Eve fished it out.

"My pony!" cried Priscilla. The pony was covered with cake crumbs and frosting. Otherwise it was fine.

"Your pony had the right idea," said Eve. "He took one look at Felicity, and he hid."

That evening Priscilla phoned all her guests to thank them for their gifts. She thanked Stan for the football. "If you want," said Stan. "I will break it in for you." She thanked Heidi for the silver barrettes. "They will keep the hair out of your face," Heidi explained.

Finally, Priscilla phoned Felicity, "Thank you for your gift." She studied the present in the box. It was lavender. It was ruffly.

"You are not welcome," said Felicity. "I chose that dress when we were friends. It will look terrible on an enemy. Have you tried it on?"

Priscilla could not imagine how she would look in the dress. "Not yet," she said. "I will do that as soon as I hang up the phone."

"I warn you, Priscilla Robin Redbreast." Felicity sounded just like her old self. "You had better not wear that dress to dancing class or piano recitals or birthday parties or . . ."

"Felicity did her best." Priscilla's mother helped Priscilla put on the ruffly new dress.

"She tried hard to be a friend," Priscilla's father agreed.

"Rrrggrr," growled Pow-wow.

Eve looked up from the pumpkin she was carving. "Felicity told me she prefers fighting to friendship."

"I don't mind." Priscilla stood still while her mother buttoned the buttons. "As a friend, Felicity is a washout. As an enemy, she is the best there is." Priscilla pranced her glass pony through the air.

"Stand still while I tie the sash," said her mother. "There. Let's see."

Priscilla skittered to the center of the kitchen. She slowly turned in place. Her mother studied the dress. Her father studied the dress. Eve and Pow-wow did, too.

"Wrrrooou," howled Pow-wow.

"Hmmmmmm," said Priscilla's father. "Most unusual."

Priscilla examined her reflection in the kitchen's sliding glass door. Giant lavender ruffles exploded from the tops of her socks to the tip of her nose.

"Perhaps if I took it in a bit," said Priscilla's mother.

"That dress looks as though it is eating you," said Eve.

"Felicity wanted me to promise never to wear it," explained Priscilla. "But I said no."

"No?" said her father.

"No?" said her mother and Eve.

"No," repeated Priscilla. To see what it felt like just once, she fluffed her ruffles. "I told Felicity this is the perfect dress for one special occasion—"

"Rrrrrggr," Pow-wow growled at Eve's jack-o-lantern.

"That's right," said Priscilla, "Halloween!"

KATHLEEN LEVERICH has been a children's book editor and an editor of *Cricket* magazine. Her stories for adult readers have appeared in magazines here and abroad. This is her third book for children. Ms. Leverich and her husband live in Somerville, Massachusetts.

SUSAN CONDIE LAMB was born and grew up in Connecticut. She graduated from Kenyon College in 1981 with a B.A. in Fine Arts, and she received an M.F.A. from Yale University in 1985. Ms. Lamb lives and works in New York City.